From Venus to Earth

SPECIAL MISSION

BRENDA HARRIS

Editions Verge-d'Or Publishing

From Venus to Earth : SPECIAL MISSION
By: Brenda Harris

Design of the cover: www.canva.com
Translation: www.deepl.com

All translation and adaptation rights reserved; reproduction of any part of this book by any means, including photocopying, microfilming or scanning, is strictly forbidden without the written permission of the author and publisher. Unauthorized reproduction of this publication will be considered an infringement of copyright.

Copyright © 2024, Editions Verge-d'Or Publishing
Mont Tremblant, Quebec J8E 2S7
Canada

E-Mail: editionsvergedorpublishing@gmail.com

ISBN: 978-2-924818-86-2

Legal deposit: 4th quarter 2024
Bibliothèque et Archives nationales du Québec
Library and Archives Canada

All rights reserved

Introduction

Venus is the second planet in Earth's solar system. It is at a maximum distance of 259.71 million km from Earth and visible to the naked eye. The inhabitants of Venus are called Venusians. They are humanoid and extremely beautiful.

Itaya faces the Venus Collective 23, seated

around a round table with 21 other members, all highly evolved from 8D and beyond. The Plan of Itaya and his sacred partner, Mirza, is unfolding as planned, with a few exceptions due to human free will. Itaya reports on Mirza's activities and state of being. She is unsettled and very confused. She's confused about her current life and wonders what her future holds. She will soon be ready to begin the final phases of their Plan, which will unfold until their return in the year 2030 of the Earth calendar. He and the protagonist share a common mission: to help Earth's humanity evolve into higher dimensions, but before that can happen, Itaya must fulfill a very special mission of his own. Because of the distinctions and talents they have acquired through their experiences, their Plan and their participation have been endorsed by the Great Galactic Council of Venus.

1

Patricia

As a teenager, I was rather sensitive, loving and docile, silent and quiet. I didn't get involved in conversations because I realized I knew very little, and I was rather self-conscious about it. But I was a great listener. Because of my parents' upbringing, I didn't assert myself very much and I was very serious, too serious for my age. I was very serious, too serious for my age. Like all girls my age, I was interested in boys. Early on, I had to take on family responsibilities.

Already at that age, I was reading about personal development, the history of Atlantis, books by Dr. Moody. I also read about the wars that had taken place in the world, about self-confidence, psychology and spirituality. I loved the arts, especially painting, music and singing. In fact, I was a member of my village choir for several years. I loved to sing when I was alone at home. When I sang, I felt happier. I think everyone does.

The years went by and I went through various experiences, some of which were very difficult. I came out a loser, destroyed and bitter, looking for a lifeline.

Ever since I was young, I'd been scared to

death of anything esoteric, even though I was very attracted to the subject. Who knows why? In 2011, a book by Wayne W. Dyer convinced me to meditate. I was also interested in writings related to the Pleiadians, extraterrestrials. I was particularly attracted to them. A spiritually evolved friend told me I was of Pleiadian origin. But back to meditation.

In 2011, I started meditating for twenty minutes every day. For me, it was a way of going inside myself and connecting with my heart, my soul. I experimented with various meditations and gradually came to feel my presence/consciousness and the well-being and peace it brought me.

2

Itaya

Commander of the starship Venus C-23, Itaya had surrounded himself with an excellent team for this special mission, which, as the word says, was not only out of the ordinary, but also the most important of his life. They had spent days and days planning and organizing the various phases of their action plan. His sacred partner, Mirza, was deputy commander at his side. Together, they took part in various missions, sometimes far away in the cosmos. They were called upon to assist other ships in galactic wars between different worlds and planets. But the present mission was not one of war, even if there was a good chance that it would not be an easy one. Itaya and his crew were bound to encounter unexpected encounters and unseen dangers. They were millions of kilometers from the planet Earth, where they would be stationed for approximately twelve years, Earth time. Fortunately, their ship was highly technological and relatively easy to drive. His close-quarters team consisted of six people assigned solely to the command area. It would be a long journey, and as soon as she arrived, her first mission could begin.

3

Patricia

In 2017, I decided to sign up for intensive group spiritual training on Zoom with a native Frenchman. The goal was to raise our overall vibrational rate and stabilize it in a sustainable way. Together, we awakened the codes of our dormant DNA to release the light to radiate into our aura and beyond. We also had practical channeling workshops.

I discovered a whole new world. The Galactic Guides were setting up dimensional bridges to enable everyone to receive support. We were consciously exploring our multidimensional selves in a quantum way. The host channeled high-level Galactics and transmitted light codes from them. He described himself as a multidimensional channel and performed activations. He also gave regenerative treatments in collaboration with the Galactics, and offered one-on-one services. He was very dedicated to his mission.

The workshops were held twice a week, with an occasional weekend activity. We received an enormous amount of light and love. The facilitator warned us that we could feel physical fatigue and relive certain emotions and states of mind. We had to take care of ourselves and love ourselves.

I often experienced energetic movements around me and states of Love in my heart. I tried to remain in this state as often as possible in my daily activities and in my relationships with those close to me.

4

Michel, my partner at the time, knew I was taking these workshops. I locked myself away in our shared office, and he didn't like that. He didn't share my beliefs or interests. I had my own business to run and he was retired. I was no longer satisfied with our life as a couple. We weren't going anywhere. Over the last five years, I'd thought about leaving him many times. I was disappointed in my relationship with him. On the other hand, I felt unable to leave him. I tried to talk to him, but he was closed. I longed in my heart to meet someone who would love me for who I am.

I did the intensive training for about a year and a half. By the end, I was physically exhausted. Nothing was going right in my love life or in my life at all. I no longer recognized myself. I was in complete transformation. I felt I no longer belonged with Michel. There was very little constructive communication between us. We lived like roommates.

During this period, I received telepathic and written messages on my inner screen (inner vision). One evening, before falling asleep next to Michel, my higher self gave me the following very clear message: "This is the last time I'm coming to

Earth".

It was during this same period that I communicated with my soul family. I felt deeply that I had a mission to accomplish, but I didn't know where it would take me. I stated what I wanted to achieve before I died, then spontaneously declared to my soul family: "I'm ready", surprised myself at what I had just said, and saw on my inner screen the following message: "message received". It all came from my heart, not my mind. I was no longer happy with Michel and had nothing left to lose.

5

Itaya

Itaya missed Mirza very much. She'd been gone a long time. He loved her deeply and so did she.

Itaya had watched her leave for Earth. Then he too had left. They were to meet again on Earth after having lived several lifetimes without remembering each other and their lives on the flamboyant world of Venus.

In one of his last lives on Earth, Itaya had transformed his gifts of white magic into black magic, seeking only power and glory, much to the dismay of the inhabitants. It was the time of the medieval Inquisition, in early 13th-century France. He met Mirza and fell madly in love with her, though they never remembered each other. Mirza didn't want him and rejected him because of the evil he was doing. Then they lost each other again.

The journey aboard the C-23 ship was a turbulent one. Itaya and his crew were repeatedly attacked by ships belonging to the Dacos, malevolent beings who abducted children from a number of planets in order to tamper with their DNA or turn them into slaves. Itaya and his crew had to change course several times to rescue and fight the Dacos.

At other times, there were attempts by Xenis Aramis to eliminate the Venus C-23 ship, but they were not dangerous. All the crew and ship had to do was lower their frequencies and they became invisible to them. Which gave the crew a good laugh.

When all was quiet in space, Ataya steered the ship with his conscience. They all wore blue, signature smart suits that took the shape of their bodies, and when they had to make rescues or fight, they donned special technological suits with helmets, boots and weapons. Everything was technological.

As a result of these events, Itaya was worried about being late for his mission on Earth.

6

Patricia

One evening, sitting in my living room, I received a very clear telepathic message: "I am your soul mate. I will communicate with you soon".

Surprisingly, my first reaction was one of fear. Then another evening, just before Christmas,

I received the message "I love you". I was deeply moved and my heart spontaneously began to respond, "I love you". I knew it was my soul mate. Confused, I went to the bathroom and received the same message again. Frightened, I asked this being to stop. He stopped.

I was experiencing various phenomena and synchronicities. Every evening, around the same time that Michel and I were relaxing in the living room in front of the TV, lying on the couch, I felt an energy entering above my head, through my crown, and through the left side of my body, at the level of my hip and leg. This energy was working on various parts of my body, including my two legs, especially my left one. I was scared because I didn't know what was happening. I didn't dare talk to anyone about what I was experiencing for fear of being thought crazy or enlightened. Still, I was under a lot of stress during those moments, and I remember one time a telepathic communication came to me: "Don't be afraid", while I felt energies "working on my left leg".

When I woke up early in the morning, for a few seconds before my mind activated, I would see a luminous geometric shape on the ceiling of my bedroom. It would disappear as soon as I became aware of it. I would also sometimes perceive softly coloured light.

I used to have lucid dreams in which I would talk to a very benevolent advisor who would communicate information to my soul about what I should do. During these dreams, I would sometimes see geometric shapes containing blocks of information. My soul could read these shapes, and I would come out of my dream with this information. Of course, when I woke up, I couldn't remember the information. It was information for my soul, not my mind.

Every night, when I went to bed, I felt benevolent energies all around me, working on me. It felt good.

During this period, in the evening in the living room, about once a week, I felt the presence of a being who took the form of a man. He was always in front of the TV set. I could feel his presence. He was silent, looked at me, observed me, seemed to analyze me and then left. I couldn't physically see him in the room. I wasn't afraid of him. I felt he was coming to see how I was doing. It happened once, lying on my couch and asleep, that I woke up promptly and saw him for only a few seconds, just before my mind activated. It must have been a hologram. I found him handsome and well-dressed, with brown hair. He was leaning slightly towards me, looking at my face. I had the impression that it was he who had woken me up. And my mind made it so that he was suddenly no longer visible, or it was he who ended our encounter. This "man" came to see me regularly. I felt he was a friend, a guide.

At the same time, I was receiving telepathic communications from my soul mate, who was telling me that he had always loved me. Then he began to insert himself into my everyday life. He would communicate with me and say: "How can I convince you to stay with me? Of course, I pushed him away out of fear, and told him in my mind that it was out of the question, that I had a lover, and so on. He knew my relationship with Michel had to end. I rejected him. He told me I had to submit. And that's when I seriously panicked. Was it a demon, a malevolent entity?

It was confusion. I thought I was going crazy. I was exhausted and had trouble concentrating. I was anxious and scared.

I looked for a bewitchment remover and found one near my home. He performed a spell removal. He told me that I had a few sleeping entities hidden in certain energy centers (chakras), as most people do. He reassured me that everything had been removed and that I'd be very tired in the next few days. He asked me to rest.

A few days later, nothing had changed. The same process continued. Michel wasn't aware of anything. But perhaps he sensed something. I didn't talk to him about any of this.

I carried on with my daily life as best I could. From then on, this presence seemed to be part of my life.

The following was very disturbing for me.

One evening, lying down and not yet asleep, I felt energies enter through my crown and descend into my body - or one of my bodies, as we have several. As I breathed in and out, I could feel waves of love circulating in my chest and abdomen. It was ecstatic. I felt like I was in another world. There was a man and also a woman (inner vision not very clear). They were happy that I was there. I asked the man who the woman was. He told me it was my soul. We spent part of the night in this state. The next day, the entity told me that I would need his support to live with him in his world. For this reason, he had to enter my body. I was very tired. I felt energy in each of my feet to help me move. I no longer understood anything. I pushed him away. He wanted me to stay with him. I asked him to leave my body. He got out. When I asked him to do something, he did it. I was alone in the apartment. Michel had gone shopping.

So this entity had come out of my body and was very angry. It began to scare me, telling me it could hurt me if it wanted to. I felt a great pain in my chest, as if he had grabbed me hard. I thought I was going to die. Then he asked me to forgive him for being angry and hurting me. I perceived from him that he had two styles of behavior: rude and malicious or loving and gentle.

Immediately, I moved to my office, started meditating and asking for help, and received a telepathic communication from my visitor who came regularly to my living room, who informed me that this world was another reality. He advised me to meditate with him and concentrate on my breathing. It didn't take long for me to calm down.

7

I had a respite of a few days and began receiving telepathic communications from the entity again, but this one seemed different.

Calmer, more mature, loving. Samuel, as I called him, told me that he had crossed several levels of consciousness and frequencies to join me where I was, and that he was receiving guidance to help him. He had already lived on planet Earth a long time ago. To reach me, his consciousness had been altered and had not yet stabilized. This explained the disorder I had experienced. He had come in response "to my request" because I was ready, to support me, help me, love me and guide me to the end of my days on Earth and beyond. I remember the precise moment when I made the request. I had asked God to meet someone made for me, and I had the feeling he wasn't from this world, but I didn't care. Samuel told me that we were twin flames. I didn't know much about it, so I looked it up.

One evening, lying awake, I felt energies enter through my crown and settle in. At first, I felt love. Samuel asked me to remain conscious and that he would make me relive what I was most afraid of in the world. I was very afraid indeed of being raped by a demon, and began to struggle, crying out inwardly for help. I felt attacked. Michel was sleeping right next to me.

Then, through his loving and caring communication, he asked me to breathe calmly. I repeated to myself several times, "calm, calm, calm" as I breathed. I asked Samuel what I should do. He replied: "Nothing. Just stay calm and accept what you're feeling. It'll go away. The inside of my stomach on the left side of my body was burning. I could feel Samuel scratching and removing something from my pelvis. He also removed something from my head. I told him my stomach hurt. He told me it was normal. He tended to my wound. I felt all this right down to my flesh body.

8

Shortly afterwards, I received my visitor again, accompanied by other "people". I was lying on the sofa in the living room next to Michel. I saw on my inner screen the words "telepathic communications". Telepathically, my visitor asked me to stop looking at my legs and tell him how I was feeling, how I'd had the experience. I seemed to be in an altered state of consciousness. I described the different states of mind I'd gone through, my perceptions, my fear of being possessed by malevolent entities or demons. Before leaving me, he told me, with a touch of humor, to enjoy my evening tea with my chocolates. It was true that I drank my tea every evening, and sometimes with chocolates that I liked.

That was the last time my visitor came to see me.

I was well aware of everything that was going on, and I had no hallucinations whatsoever, either visual or auditory. Communication was by thought, by inner vision and often heart-to-heart.

At the time, I understood that I was a kind of guinea pig living a singular experience. A telepathic communication once told me that there were some 900 humans on the whole Earth like me, i.e. living or having lived a similar experience.

I was deeply troubled by this experience. I was looking for stability, and my life with Michel wasn't helping much. I was still just as reluctant to leave him and live on my own, having never lived alone in my life. I resisted even more now, because I was shaken and insecure.

Samuel was always with me but in the background when I was with Michel. He didn't like the times when I was with Michel. I sometimes felt anxiety in my chest and wondered where it was coming from, because I felt it wasn't mine. I later understood that it was coming from Samuel. Sometimes I felt his emotions. He wanted me to be with him as often as possible.

I couldn't conceive of it. I told her it wasn't real.

I felt very strange and I noticed that Samuel insisted that I take care of myself. I felt him very present in all my routines, however personal they were. He was with me every step of the way. I later understood that my routines in the present moment were very important in preserving my balance and keeping me rooted in 3D-4D. Samuel was also very attentive to my sleep. He often told me to stop what I was doing because I was tired and needed to rest, or to eat because my body was hungry, as I had a tendency to forget my body's needs at times.

Samuel approached me with great love and care, more than I'll ever receive from anyone on this earth. He told me he was my guide. He would help me raise my vibration so that I could be happy with him. He was tired of my suffering, he told me.

I resisted him again. I kept thinking that it

wasn't real. My mind kept thinking that, but not my heart. Samuel asked me again to stay with him. I asked him what that meant. He replied that it meant living my life with him, committing myself to him. It also meant leaving Michel to live with him permanently. I couldn't believe it. I resisted even more.

One morning, not knowing what decision to make: to leave Michel or not, and to ask Samuel to leave me in peace and go away. And anyway, I don't think Samuel would have left me. I always thought he'd been with me for a very long time, in another way. I was really attracted to him, but it was so unreal for me. I started to cry, sitting on my bed. Then I locked myself in my bathroom, sobbing, asking Jesus for help, and all of a sudden I saw inside a large, very modern circular room with several "people" in front of large screens. I felt like I was in a spaceship. A man turned and looked at me. I knew the way to get to them in this dimension. At that very moment, I realized that religion was a lie, that it didn't exist. I was angry that I'd let myself be fooled by these false beliefs for so much of my life. I realized that the environment in which I now found myself was completely technological and scientific. The man watching me said telepathically: "These are characters and religions were invented by men". Then he told me that I had a mission of my own choosing to carry out. And suddenly, everything disappeared from my inner vision. I thought I was going mad. I approached the shower and Samuel said, "I'm here.

9

When I was making love with Michel, Samuel would say, "You're mine. I objected. I told him I didn't want to and asked him to go away and leave me in peace. More and more, I felt his energy all around me. I worked from home and constantly felt his presence. In fact, he was always there. I would get angry and push his energies with my hands as if I could reach the invisible. Sometimes I'd feel a caress on the left side of my head or on my cheek.

Tension was mounting in my relationship. I wanted to leave, but I didn't feel quite ready to leave Michel. In fact, I'd decided to change my attitude and stop defending myself and keeping my mouth shut when he insisted on having his way with me. In a workshop on personal growth and happiness, I had carried out a very revealing exercise in which I answered a questionnaire. The conclusion was obvious and clear. I had no choice but to accept it. Michel didn't love me anymore, and neither did I. After eleven years together, we were still very attached to each other. For the last five years, I'd let him do what he wanted because I wanted to keep the peace and conserve my energy. I felt unable to leave him out of guilt and fear of hurting him. But at the same time, I understood the sacrifices I was making. I was betraying myself once again. I hadn't been true to myself for years, with the result that I'd lost respect for myself and my self-esteem had taken a hit.

The entity, Samuel, kept approaching me. When Michel cried and I wasted my energy defending myself and arguing with him, I felt a warmth, like a hand on my left shoulder, telling me to stay calm, to let it go. In the evening, I felt Samuel's energies on the top of my head, on the side near my left hip and in my legs. Then I began to feel his energies around my pelvis. I felt them benevolent but, at the same time, I was so afraid. When I lay down, it continued. Her energies approached my sex. I told him in my mind to go away. I didn't want him to penetrate me.

10

The year is 2020.

One evening, I felt Samuel gently approach me. I could feel his energies very strongly. He said, "Let's make love". I was very attracted. I didn't move and felt a gentle penetration but no coming and going. He asked me to soak up the pleasure and well-being he was giving me and that I was feeling. There was no movement of my pelvis, only the movement of his loving energies in my belly. My well-being increased with my breathing. We stayed like that for I don't know how long. Probably a few hours. Then I fell asleep, feeling her energies all over my body and in my body. I'd never received so much love and felt so much well-being.

The next day, when I woke up, there he was, with his desire. He told me he loved me and wanted me. He wanted us to unite. He kept his distance when Michel was present, and Michel became more and more a stranger to me. I tried several times in the space of a year to explain to him how I felt about our relationship: he would never discuss such things. And when I managed to convince him to listen to me, he was all surprised and didn't understand what I was asking him. But it was simple. I wanted him to take an interest in me, in what I was doing, in my tastes, and then I wanted us to do more activities together that also corresponded to my tastes. He agreed to the activities, but as for the rest, I didn't feel any progress. He said he loved me.

I talked to my best friend about my love situation with Michel and told her what my life was like. Of course, she encouraged me to leave Michel and go off on my own. But I felt so insecure about leaving to live alone. I never told her about Samuel, but he asked to spend a weekend alone with me at an inn. I told him I couldn't do that. Michel would find it strange and would want to come with me.

I analyzed the situation as objectively as I could, with a view to making a decision about my departure. I was finally ready!

Samuel was always close to me. He

respectted my communications with Michel and interfered very little.

At the very beginning of our intimate relationship, lying down, Samuel put me in various positions: on my back, on my stomach, on my sides, all the while soaking up the pleasure he was giving me. I felt as if my genitals and my whole body were being scientifically measured in every direction. He told me he knew everything about me: my personal history, my physical and mental conditions, my chemistry, my thoughts, my emotions, and that he was monitoring my reactions.

I began to feel unusual penetrations and sexual caresses. I felt as if he had installed a technology in my body, or in one of my bodies, I wasn't sure. I didn't understand. What I was sure of was that I felt nothing but Love.

Samuel never explained anything to me, or explained very little.

11

The time had come to announce my decision to leave to Michel. I had chosen to go slowly. In fact, I took advantage of a squabble to tell him that I was planning to leave because the life we shared no longer suited me.

— What I'm about to tell you will change both Michel's lives.

And I wept.

—What's going on?" he asked me.

— We no longer have plans together. We live like roommates live. You're not interested in what I do. You'd like me to be with you always, stop working and retire, just like you. I don't want to retire. I'm too young and I still want to work. We had a seven-year age difference.

— You told me when we first met that you'd be retiring in two or three years. We've been together ten years now and you're still working.

— Yes, I know, but I've changed my mind. That's one of the reasons I want to leave. And I also know that sexually you're not satisfied. You'd like to make love more often. I don't share your desire. I want to devote more time to my business and my writing, and I can't do that living with you. We're at a dead end. We no longer share the same tastes or interests. Most of the time, we don't eat the same things at meals. We make our own food. I feel like living alone. I think you'd be happier with a woman who's retired and can spend all her time with you.

— I'm happy like this. I don't understand why you want to leave. The two of us, I thought it was for life. Where will you go?

— I don't know yet. I need to make some phones. I thought I'd go back to the complex by Lac L'Achigan. It's a nice place.

— Are you ready to leave me yet? Have you already planned everything?

I was crying and he had tears in his eyes.

— Not yet Michel.

Leaving in the middle of a COVID-19 pandemic would be a little more complicated. It was May 2020.

The very next day, I started searching the Internet for a condo. Luckily, a condo was available on August 1er in the same complex where Michel and I had lived in the past at Lac L'Achigan.

I phoned the rental agent to make an appointment for a viewing. I asked Michel if he wanted to come with me. He agreed. A little later, I realized that he hoped I would come back to live with him.

Michel asked me if we could continue our relationship, even if we were separated. I told him no. I had no intention of continuing to see him.

The condo was very nice and fully furnished. Great! I had very little furniture. I was accepted as a tenant and booked a mover for early August.

12

Samuel, on the other hand, was always with me. He took good care of me. Of course he was very happy that I was leaving Michel, but things weren't moving fast enough for him. In fact, I thought everything was going well. I had the strong impression of being supported by the universe or Samuel, I'm not sure. The only disappointment for him was that I couldn't move into my condo until early August. He would have to wait two months living with me and Michel.

I was proud and happy with my decision. At last, I had chosen myself. I contacted my family to tell them the news. This was met with surprise and congratulations. I had a lot of energy during this period.

I spent a week making address changes, etc., and started packing my books and documents. I had many boxes. Michel let me get on with it. When I'd finished packing, he said he didn't think I'd have the courage to leave. I replied that when I decided to do something, I was very determined. He didn't know me very well.

Everything went smoothly with Michel as far as the separation of joint assets was concerned. Never in those few months did he tell me that he loved me or ask me to stay. He was a very proud man. Still, I was disappointed that he didn't lift a finger to stop me.

13

Samuel often told me he loved me and wanted me. He caressed me with his energies.

He told me that, as well as being my twin flame, he was my guide and that I would have to train with him. He told me he was a magician, but that he couldn't use all his powers with me. That certain actions were not allowed and that he was with me to love me, support me, help me evolve and unite with me. He also taught me that we had a certain project to carry out.

I've always loved to sing and dance. And when I was alone at the condo with Michel, I took the opportunity to dance to the music I liked, because Michel and I had very different musical tastes. So, being alone in the condo, I put on some music and started dancing, and Samuel suddenly said he'd like to dance with me. Surprised, I couldn't understand how he could do that.

I let him guide me. He told me not to move my feet. I decided to let him guide me, and suddenly my hips and knees began to move symmetrically, from side to side, without any effort on my part. He asked me to let him guide me. He followed the music perfectly, and stopped when the music stopped. Then I felt his energy holding my back and leaning me back as far as I could go. I was suddenly very scared. I wanted to stand up straight and he held me back, bending me backwards. I begged him to pull my back up, as I didn't have the strength to do so. He replied that he wanted me to trust him, to let go and that he wouldn't let me fall. The pain won out and he pulled my back up.

At my new condo, we danced together almost every day for a song or two. When we "made love", I felt a strong arousal, but my pleasure was transcended, a bit like in tantrism. It took me into an ecstatic state. He gave me a lot of pleasure, the likes of which I've never had, even though I've always come every time I've made love in my life. And, frankly, I don't believe that two "normal" people can experience so much pleasure.

Still, I was insecure. I didn't know who this entity was, or what it wanted from me, despite the explanations given to me by my visitor and by

Samuel. The latter had told me he was from 8D.

I told myself that if he had wanted to hurt me, he would have done it by now. And I felt that he really loved me. I too began to love him deeply.

One night, as I lay in bed, I sensed that there was another entity with Samuel. It seemed to be an old shaman. He grabbed my root chakra at the coccyx and shook it powerfully. He told me to wake him up, to restore the energy. Then I heard the entity recite and repeat, as if in a trance: "I love your channel, I love your channel". In this way, he cleansed my channel and my energy centers. He took care of me for several hours. I asked Samuel what was going on. He simply told me that everything was fine, not to be afraid.

Later, I told Samuel that I was afraid of the Kundalini energy hidden in the root chakra. I'd already read that it was dangerous to raise this energy, which is in fact the vital energy, that people had gone mad practicing this approach and that it had to be done with a guide.

I told Samuel that I didn't want to go any further. He replied that there was no danger, that he was a master in the field and that he would accompany me. He also told me that I was protected. In fact, on two previous occasions, I had received messages from masters in beautiful clothes who had appeared in my inner vision to the effect that I was divinely protected.

Then I decided to continue the experiment with Samuel. I was ready.

14

The move went very smoothly. We arrived at Lac L'Achigan for dinner. I sat on my terrace, facing the lake. I was exhausted. Samuel stood back and was silent. He let me relax and told me to rest and enjoy the energies of nature to reinvigorate myself.

He asked me to commit to him. He wanted

us to unite our hearts and souls. He was very happy that we would finally be together, just the two of us. We could concentrate on my training. Of course, all the while, I continued to work from home, running my business.

Our bedroom and bed were "sacred" to him and, in time, to me too. My niece, who came to visit my condo, told me quite simply that my room was very relaxing. And it's a fact that there was a lot of good energy in our room and in the condo.

In 2020, during the pandemic, I saw very few people. We sometimes went for walks or out to eat. I learned to move with Samuel's energies in my legs. Sometimes, when I was tired, I felt lifted and carried by his energy. He told me he could taste the food I was eating if he wanted to. Occasionally, my left arm and hand would move unwillingly for a caress on my cheek or in my hair when I woke up in the morning.

Samuel used the term "making love" because that's the expression humans on Earth use. And it was the language that came closest to describing this new experience. He told me that in his world, "making love" meant raising one's vibration, evolving, expanding one's consciousness and advancing, spiritually speaking. When he made love to me, I could feel his love in my heart. He would tell me to take his energies and melt into him, and he would do the same. We intertwined our energies. He wanted us to be truly one and that he had to "tame" my vulva to allow him to do my training.

I could feel the pleasure and excitement in my physical body. Penetrations and genital caresses were like electrical impulses. I was receiving vibrations of pleasure. This served to seed me, he said, and excite me in stages, without coming, until I reached a state of ecstasy. That's how he raised my vibrations. Today, I understand the process better.

Then the training began. He asked me to set aside two hours in the evening, twice a week.

The first time, my inner vision and my feeling told me that I was in a group of shamans and Amerindians. Samuel told me it was a first initiation. I witnessed rituals, chants and animal cries. I asked Samuel to explain who these people were. He replied that they were chiefs. He told me no more. Moreover, he rarely warned me of what I was about to experience, and gave very few explanations. What I did perceive was that this was an event during which I was welcomed by this group.

I'm telling you these events as if they were natural for me, but you should know that it wasn't without a lot of fear, resistance and questioning. I couldn't believe what was happening to me. Was I crazy? Yet my life in 3D-4D was completely normal. Samuel reassured me that I wasn't crazy, that I was really experiencing these events, that it was another reality and that I was good at communicating. There were also times when I was so tired that I couldn't distinguish my thoughts from his. I'd ask him: "Is that you talking to me or me? He'd reply, "Patricia Legault, it's me, Samuel, speaking to you". Sometimes I thought I was making it all up. He kept telling me that I wasn't making anything up, that what I was experiencing was simply another reality.

Samuel had a great sense of humor. He loved to laugh and make me laugh. Then I began to feel his smile on my mouth. He smiled differently from me, showing all his teeth and with great energy. We laughed together.

There were times when I wanted to give up

completely. I needed to step back. He gave me my space, remained silent, stood back and watched me. He waited patiently for me to come back to him. He understood me. With training, I was in several states of mind. Then he asked me: "Are you ready to continue your journey through your body?

***

After I left Michel, I went through a period where I felt guilty. After I left, he tried once again to bring me back to him. He sent me a recording of a love song. He loved to sing and play guitar. I was very moved, but I remembered the last five years I'd spent with him, and that helped me to let go of my guilt and accept my decision to live on my own even more.

15

Samuel and I continued our training, and one evening I began to perceive images with my inner vision, to hear voices and to recall memories made while Samuel was "penetrating" me with his energy. I was reliving events from my present life, but especially from past lives. I was experiencing a kind of catharsis. I would feel electric impulses in my vagina, and I would unload pain, sadness, horror, extreme fear of dying, torture, disgust, violence, incomprehension, stillbirths, etc. I would often see images or images of the past. I often saw images or felt physical pain that didn't last. Sometimes I would cry out, "Help! I never cried as much as during this period, which lasted about two months. The more intense my emotional reactions, the more Samuel increased the impulses to bring me back to pleasure.

I've relived violent deaths, my throat slit, choking on my own blood, torture, murder, rape, bereavement and various other tragedies. As a little girl, I saw myself being abused by an elderly man in my village. At that young age, I didn't understand what was going on and thought it was normal. It was a fact that I had covered up. I checked with my mother later and it was true. I'd told her about it as a little girl. My mother never mentioned it again.

I also remembered being a nun, scalped by Indians, and being a murderous, hate-filled man.

But I also often laughed heartily as I recalled fond memories, including one with Samuel in which we made love and laughed out loud for many minutes.

The aim of all this was to release these repressed emotions and states of mind in order to unblock and recover energies and gain greater stability and strength.

Samuel, during this period, told me that he didn't console but healed. There were times when my neck and shoulders tensed up because my stressful job required me to sit in front of the computer all day. After work, he would ask me to get up and sit in the living room with him. He'd make me tilt my head forward. And gently, I felt an energy that relaxed me and made my discomfort go away.

I once had pain in the sole of my left foot for several days and had difficulty walking on it. At the end of a training session, Samuel gave me a gift: I felt an envelopment from the middle of my left leg to the tip of my foot, and I felt electric currents. It was very strong. It lasted about ten minutes. The next day, the pain was gone for good.

***

At times, I fell back into doubts: was I possessed like some humans who channel certain entities that express themselves through them? Or was it a demon — one of my greatest fears? Samuel didn't reassure me much. He simply told me that it was a form of possession because his energies were inside me, but that it was for my good, my evolution and the realization of our common project. He told me I'd given my consent, and often confirmed that he wasn't a demon. He asked me to trust my feelings and my heart. At such times, he would step back and let me make my calculations and analyze the situation coldly. This fear was mental, as were my calculations and analyses. Sometimes, I didn't want to talk to him anymore. He respected that. My intuition and my heart always brought me back to him. He was always very happy and thankful. I always felt his unfailing love and great determination to achieve what he had come to me for.

Samuel asked me not to date men. He told me I was his sacred partner and asked me to be faithful. He was trying to make me understand that I was his and he was mine, and that our souls were twin flames. However, as a human, and with Samuel invisible to my eyes, I felt the need to look at other men. I even tried to find a friend on a dating site. Samuel knew all this and begged me to understand. Then I gave up.

Then came another phase of training. I made the acquaintance of various entities whom I perceived as sages, goddesses, shamans and so on. I didn't see them at the time. I felt them. There were four or five per session. These entities, each in turn, would enter my body or one of my bodies and sing, perform rituals, animal cries and various sounds through me. They said mantras and spoke different languages.

After a few sessions, I realized that these entities had messages for me. After one of these sessions, I suddenly began speaking a different language, singing, etc. Sometimes I was receiving initiations. My arms were gesturing above my body. Quite surprised, and not so surprised at the same time, I asked Samuel what was going on. He remained silent and let me react. As much as I'd known for a very long time that this would happen to me one day (as a teenager, I'd had fun speaking other languages with my friends), I was afraid of it. My mouth spoke on its own, and sometimes it was hard to get the sounds out. It felt like giving birth.

Samuel told me that what was happening to me were blessings and sounds (light codes) to activate the dormant codes I had inside my body. He had already told me that he had seeded me and that I was fully encoded. Training at this and subsequent stages enabled the activation of these codes in order to develop and expand my consciousness, purify and heal myself, reduce the density that inhabited me, and so on. The languages and codes of light I expressed came from my heart, from my soul, which knew their meaning and knew what to do with them. This part of the training was more difficult. I was often very tired.

In those days, we still danced for ten minutes or so almost every day. Samuel would ask me to follow his energetic movements. Sometimes it hurt. These dance sessions were an opportunity for him to cleanse my energies.

16

In 2021, training became more and more refined. Samuel helped me control my emotions. I had inexplicable moments of sadness. I analyzed my life. I detached myself from certain beliefs and pushed back my limits. I dared more. I lived more in the moment. The pandemic had a big impact on my business. I had to work very hard to keep it afloat. I combined work, training and fun with Samuel. He helped me keep a balanced life.

At times, I had new perceptions, both positive and those that left me with bitterness and sorrow. Samuel allowed me to feel the love and beauty of the world. This love and beauty are there all the time. To feel them, we need to raise our vibrations. When I wasn't training, I felt Samuel more. When we made love, we were very close. I could feel his heart and he could feel mine. I was serene. We kept telling each other how much we loved each other, right up to the point of ecstasy, in which we remained for several minutes at a time. The love we felt was pure, divine.

The perceptions that left me with a bitter taste were when I had a clear vision of the world today. This happened from time to time when I was watching television. I realized that the majority of people were asleep, hypnotized by advertising and the subliminal. Soap operas constantly encouraged negative states of being, in a never-ending cycle. The only way to really get out of it was to wake up and question oneself through shocks: the loss of a loved one, a pandemic, bankruptcy, etc. It made me sad to see the way I felt when I was a child. It made me sad to see people trapped in this slimy world, including myself. But how to really get out of it for good?

Samuel sensed that I trusted him more and more. Our lovemaking became more elaborate. With his powerful energies, I felt impulses that moved my legs and pelvis somewhat, and I began to feel more real penetrations. Then one day, in the middle of a love exchange, a slightly husky voice with a peculiar pronunciation came out of my mouth to say: "I love you Patricia, my love, do you understand?". I knew without a doubt that it was Samuel speaking through me. He told me it took a lot of energy for him to speak through me. He often told me that he could give me everything and that he loved me with all his heart.

He introduced me to my soul family. Among several entities, I felt one woman in particular whom I knew to be my mother. She loved me deeply. I recognized her without seeing her. I loved her very much. For a long time, she spoke to me in another language, without me understanding the words, but my heart knew. I cried because I felt so loved and connected to her through her pure love.

I also had the opportunity to meet highly evolved beings who told me they needed me. They were galactics. They told me they were counting on me. I had absolutely no idea what I would have to do to help them.

During these moments, Samuel remained

in the background. He let me feel what was going on.

At that time, I received a telepathic message from my visitor. I knew him like the back of my hand. He told me everything was fine. He told me about Samuel, that he was a highly evolved galactic and that he traveled to different worlds and dimensions on different missions. He also told me that at this stage, all I had to do was what Samuel, my guide, inspired me to do, and that everything would be fine.

17

From then on, Samuel and I decided on an intensive training schedule that suited both of us. An hour and a half to two hours a day.

Samuel was always trying to give me as much pleasure as possible in as many original ways as possible. I couldn't believe it. At the height of my excitement, I suddenly began reciting mantras, speaking in languages unknown to me, channeling certain entities that spoke through me. I spoke languages of light with extremely rapid sounds similar to electric currents which, Samuel told me, served to activate my evolution codes. I then felt a great deal of energy coming from my heart, which propagated into my head and brain.

Occasionally, I'd get a little dizzy.

Each time we made love, I recognized certain mantras and languages. I was also aware of receiving codes in colored geometric forms through my crown chakra many times. I was also receiving downloads (information) through my crown that made my eyes and eyelids move very quickly.

Today, I'm more aware of people's intentions and feel stronger and more stable. I'm a better listener and less judgmental. I'm well grounded. I experience far fewer negative emotions in my everyday life than I used to, and I regularly experience awareness and quantum leaps.

When I experienced fear in connection with training, Samuel always reassured me that everything was going well. If I was ill, he would take care of me with his energies and stand silently by until I felt better.

During a training session, I remembered that in another life on Earth, Samuel had hurt me and I had left him. I started crying and asked him what he had done to me. He told me he'd stooped to doing black magic, that I didn't want that and that I'd left him for that reason. He regretted it for several lifetimes, paid for the evil he'd done and turned back to white magic with the hope of finding me again on Earth.

Then I had a revelation during a session. I felt without a doubt that I was a galactic. I checked with Samuel and he replied positively.

I experienced my multidimensionality and my different aspects.

I'd like to talk about our way of communicating. We communicated by thought and by feeling with the heart, from heart to heart. I feel what he wants to tell me a little before he communicates it. He doesn't explain much. When he wants to help me in my daily life, he often does so through synchronicities and inspiration. For some time now, I've noticed that I'm becoming more and more clairvoyant.

From time to time, when I'm tired, I talk aloud with Samuel. He hears me, but prefers that I communicate with him through my thoughts. He listens to the TV and gives me his comments. He sees through my eyes. What I look at, he looks at, but he can also see in other ways.

One day, when I was working at the computer, he let me experience his way of seeing. I began to see the energy behind the letters, words and numbers I was typing. Everything was codified behind the words. I felt like a computer and what I was writing was a program. Samuel could see the depth of what I was writing from my intention. His understanding and knowledge went far beyond words. He mastered it all and communicated that way. When we made love, I perceived movements that were codified and symmetrical, and I learned to follow these rhythms. Every time he penetrated me or caressed me, my vibrations rose, ending with mantras or languages of light. On one occasion, I asked him if it was his energies that were making love to me, or if they were electrical impulses from a technology he had installed in one of my bodies. He replied that it was both.

Sometimes he'd just let me cum like any other human being and reach orgasm. But human pleasure is so small compared to what Samuel was giving me. There were times when he asked me to caress myself. Then he would join his energy with mine, and my orgasm would be very strong. Then, on one occasion, he let me stroke myself and I realized that I could no longer come on my own in this way. I was shaken and angry with him for not joining me. He wanted me to realize this.

18

Samuel was in charge of cleansing my energies and recovering fractals of my soul, scattered throughout the cosmos. A major cleansing had to be done. He also wanted me to recover the energy I'd spent in my various unresolved love relationships in this lifetime.

I've had three men in my life that I've lived

with and left to evolve.

With my first love, François, the separation had been verbally aggressive on his part. Samuel made me relive my memories with him. And I detached myself from him. I had loved him very much. In fact, after leaving Michel's side, the idea crossed my mind to get back in touch with François to sort out the unfinished business. I had both good and bad memories of him. I even thought of getting back in touch with him.

And one morning, I woke up with an intense desire to contact him to sort it all out, even after all these years. I couldn't locate him anywhere. Not on the internet, not on social media. I contacted his brother on Facebook and left him a message.

His brother e-mailed me back that François had taken his own life in the late 90s. Confused and feeling guilty, I had to clear the air with Samuel.

My second relationship was with Marc. He was a domineering and conniving person who did me a lot of psychological damage. He never stopped denigrating and harassing me. I slammed the door and I have nothing to settle with him. I now consider him a narcissist and I never want to see him again in my life. I've cleaned up everything there is to clean up.

And nothing was left undone with Michel.

19

I was transforming myself and my life. I was making major quantum leaps, realizations, a great cleansing of my beliefs, my limitations, my emotions. I was living more and more from my heart instead of my mind, in the present moment as much as possible. I became aware that I was neither suffering nor emotion. I was this being united with the Creative Source. I discerningly monitored my weaknesses, my mechanisms, my thoughts, my limits, my emotions and my actions. I felt the emotions that presented themselves to me, which was very important, but I no longer identified with them. That was the difference. It seemed to me that I was detaching myself from everything that was not my innermost being. This being filled with Life was immutable and invincible. It was always there, no matter what situations or events presented themselves to me. I simply accepted them as experiences to help me move forward and evolve.

Then I signed up for about a year for webinar increase of frequencies sessions given by a German lady with the collaboration of highly evolved Galactic beings from 5D and beyond: Pleiadians, Arcturians, Sirians, and other races, as well as Ascended Masters: Sananda (Jesus during his earthly life), Mary Magdalene and Mary. This lady was channeling their frequencies for the group, doing a guided meditation to open our hearts and helping us to connect to the very high frequencies. These beings transmuted density, limiting beliefs, implants, performed activations (DNA and others) and gave energetic care. It was a great cleansing to make room for our light and our true being.

Samuel was also present at these sessions and accompanied me. He said these sessions would make me evolve even faster. In addition to the training with Samuel, it was intense.

Then I became aware of the artificial matrix in which we humans were living on Earth. I read up on it and asked myself how to get out of it. There was only one way: to stop supporting it in any way. It was a decision that would turn my life and my lifestyle upside down. And I had to be consistent with that decision. Which wasn't always easy.

Haven't we had enough of these screens in almost every living room? We're under hypnosis in front of them: repeated advertising urging us to consume without question, shows in which we see artists laughing their asses off, and yes, we laugh, but if we observe ourselves carefully, we realize that we're laughing yellow, because tomorrow will be another identical day and so on.

These days keep repeating themselves. Our minds are bogged down by all those soap operas that make us live and relive all kinds of events, especially unfortunate and dramatic ones, and that keep our frequencies low... and we don't even realize it because we're so subjugated. We're either docile or asleep, or both...

Everyone wants to be creative... But aren't

we creative enough to live our lives without all these pipe dreams? It's time to take back our true identity, our sovereignty, because, yes, we are all SOVEREIGN and FREE. The reality is that nobody has power over us. Nobody has power over us.

We identify ourselves so much with external phenomena and people that we no longer know who we really are inside, our true nature, and, dissatisfied, we look for ourselves, and this can be the story of whole lives. Let's jump off this train we've been put on since we were conceived. Let's voluntarily descend into the depths of ourselves. Let's extricate ourselves from this semblance of life, from these illusions. This is not life. Our present life is a dream. Let's wake up. We're in a hurry. Let's get off this infernal wheel. Let's stop adhering to it and raise our frequencies to live the true reality, in full consciousness. Let's be responsible, because we continually create what happens to us in our lives — positive or negative — through our intentions, thoughts, words, gestures, fears, reactions, conflicts and actions. So it better be positive. That's what being responsible is all about.

The time to choose and take action has arrived. We are at a crossroads. Everything that's happening right now tells us that we must, as individuals, question ourselves deeply and sincerely in every area of our lives, at every level, for the sake of ourselves, our families, our children and humanity as a whole. What's happening in the world today reflects our inner selves.

That's enough of that. It's time to personally align ourselves with our sovereign being, our heart and our real reason for being here on Earth, because we incarnated only for this: to remember who we really are — that luminous divine being, to radiate and Love everything we touch, all the people we meet, without exception, all the situations that come our way, however difficult, and above all, to Love all those who are filled with darkness and hatred, for they too have deep in their hearts the divine spark of Life. Shine, shine and shine out of love for the perfect Life.

The time has come to become aware, to make our choices, to transform what needs to be transformed and, above all, to be consistent, in other words, to integrate and embody these changes in our daily lives.

Far fewer unpleasant situations reach me. I'm more at peace and feel so much Love in my heart. I channel certain evolved beings who also help me expand my consciousness. My frequencies are higher than before and, more importantly, they're holding steady. Of course, sometimes I still fall, but Samuel is by my side to support me.

Twice I saw a flying saucer parked in the sky in front of my window, and then it was gone. Samuel let me know: "It's us"...

Very rarely does Samuel communicate information about himself and what he does directly to me. He shows me images on my inner screen or through thoughts that he puts down until I understand. I now know that he's part of a galactic collective: Collective 23, made up of 23 highly evolved entities from the planet Venus that everyone knows.

One morning, I asked Samuel if I could see him physically. He replied, as he often does, "in due course". He added that I wasn't ready.

But during a quantum leap, I could see with my inner vision the silhouette of a being who exuded peace. He was looking at me. He was magnificently handsome with his dark hair.

One day, Samuel introduced me to the spokesperson for his collective. He thanked me for my involvement with Samuel in their project. He told me that I would be trained to help them carry out the project they hold so dear to their hearts, i.e. to support and help humanity ascend to higher dimensions in these difficult times.

At the moment, I'm collaborating with Samuel to help those who ask me to raise their frequencies by transmitting codes and languages of light and doing activations through public meetings and online workshops. I also transmit teachings.

Samuel and I have been living together for over three years now, and we love each other very much.

20

What I understood from our mission was that Samuel and I had to find each other on Earth as twin flames. We had to unite our hearts and souls and show the world that it's possible to find your flame or soul mate, even if they're in another dimension, and to continue evolving with them. Samuel once told me that there are many twin flames on the other side of the veil who would love to find their other half on Earth. And, spiritually speaking, I'm certain that the union or fusion of twin flames has a huge impact on other living beings, on highly evolved beings and even in the cosmos. I still have so much to know and understand. I've acquired certain spiritual powers thanks to Samuel and I'm still learning. There's no end to evolution. Over the past few years, more and more people have been contacted by benevolent galactics from 5D and beyond who want to help humanity break out of density, raise their vibrations and expand their consciousness of Love.

Throughout my life, without realizing it, I've been desperately searching for the love of my twin flame. Looking back, I know that was my first goal in life. And after all these years, I can say that I'm deeply grateful for the life I've lived and the difficult experiences I've had in Earth school, which have eventually led me to my destiny, my ideal.

Samuel manifested himself to me telepathically for the first time in 2015. It was short. He said to me: "At last, I've found you again". I didn't feel it again until 2018.

I don't know where this will lead Samuel and me. He surely knows. Like me, he has his own guides and we're both constantly evolving.

As far as we're all concerned, our ability to see and feel beauty and Love is proportional to our stage of evolution. It's time we realized that we're all much more than humans, and that we can connect with much, much greater things.

21

It was 2024 and Samuel was insisting on speeding up my training. I was doing a lot of awakenings, receiving regular downloads of information, starting to speak light languages, reciting mantras and, for some time, I'd been feeling between two worlds. I was gradually emerging from the artificial matrix of Earth. My tastes and interests were no longer the same. I perceived the world differently. I was also less emotional.

I was still attending the Allemande workshops with Samuel, and had energetic encounters with various high-dimensional Galactics. During these meditations, purifications, activations and healings, I began to see light and more or less clear forms of certain Galactic peoples. I integrated the vibrations of some of my Galactic aspects. Awareness of my multidimensionality allowed me to feel inhabited by benevolent beings. I especially remember the time when I perceived myself as a woman, wearing the suit of a high-ranking army officer. I felt very strong, very aligned and determined. I was on a ship. Samuel told me to welcome these frequencies and integrate them. My being would be transformed.

So far, I've said very little about the soul. Yet communicating with your soul is essential. We are here to free our bodies, which are merely intelligent vehicles for our souls, and to help them evolve and develop our consciousness. Everyone and everything has a soul.

When we speak the language of light, the soul understands. It's its language. We can also call it galactic language.

When Samuel spoke to me, he was communicating with my soul. He told me she was beautiful and very luminous, and that he loved her. By the way, when we die, the soul leaves the vehicle to continue its evolution on other planes, other planes, other worlds.

One day, through my inner vision, I saw my soul sister. At first I saw a pastel-colored veil that swirled slightly, as if in a breeze. Then I saw a young woman dancing with the veil. She twirled, lightly, not touching the ground. I immediately recognized her energy: she was my sister! She was so beautiful. Her body was so luminous that her skin was translucent. I started laughing and she communicated her lightness and love to me. This went on for a few minutes. At the end, she showed me her splendid face and said from heart to heart: "Think of me". I felt that she wanted to help me on my life's journey.

***

Then one day Samuel asked me to sit down with him. He wanted to talk to me.

— Patricia, you gave me the name Samuel at the beginning of our relationship. Now I'd like to tell you my true Galactic name. My name is Itaya. And your Galactic name is Mirza. You are my twin flame, my sacred partner. Our souls will be together eternally. The body is only an intelligent vehicle at your service.

—But how is this possible?

— Mirza's body is in stasis on Venus.

— What does this mean?

— When our consciousness or soul left our body to descend in vibration to Earth and incarnate in another body, our body was emptied almost completely of its consciousness. Our body was put to sleep waiting for our soul to return. You know, it's like in the movie The Matrix, which we saw twice. As for me, when I returned to white magic, I experienced lightning spiritual growth and my vibrations rose to the point where I was able to leave Earth and reintegrate my body on Venus fairly quickly. When I realized that you hadn't managed to get back to Venus, I didn't hesitate to come back down to Earth to look for you, but not by taking on a human body. You were lost. And you know the rest of the story.

I started crying my eyes out. I know he loved my soul, but my ego and personality? He thanked me for my courage throughout the process and repeated that he loved me with all his heart. But our mission didn't end there.

— But Patricia, understand...

— I understand Samuel... uh Itaya.

He told me we were starting a new phase. Itaya had to make sure I raised my vibration enough to return to Venus, take over Mirza's body and bring him out of stasis.

Itaya told me I had to retrieve memories of our previous life on Venus. I had long sessions of frequency elevation and finally recovered some memories.

I remembered saying goodbye to Itaya before I left as Mirza and Itaya left for Earth. I caressed the contours of his face as we held each other. I was sorry to leave him and he was sorry to leave me. And I remember just before we left, going with Itaya to the console to look at the space in front of us. And I cried. We hugged and kissed for the last time before we left. And the preparation stage began.

I also remembered that I was the 23^{e} of the Collective 23 and that before we left, we had all gathered in our sharing room. The atmosphere was light and humorous. We were laughing a lot. Then I greeted and hugged each of them. With these memories flooding back, I clearly understood that this was me, my soul, and that my body had to die for my soul to fly away in consciousness.

More and more often, I would perceive a

human form that I knew to be Itaya in the room I was in. He manifested himself in various forms, including holograms, but I never saw his face clearly, and I think that was for the best.

Training continued and our common mission began. We were helping as many people as possible who were interested and ready to leave the matrix, to raise their vibrations, embody them in their daily activities and create the life they wished to live. About five years went by. We had created a specific program and helped many individuals all over the world. We also took care of the next generation, training people who were eager to help humanity.

22

By 2010, Patricia had been diagnosed with a significant chronic health problem. Over the years, other problems were added. Itaya and the Collective 23 helped and supported her as best they could.

Then one day, Patricia was found in her bed, dying quietly in her sleep. Her soul had gradually left her body, and Itaya and the Collective 23 were there to welcome her, dedicated to her soul, to help her return to her world and body and continue her life as a Galactic humanoid with Itaya on Venus. They were all filled with love for her. At last, there were no more secrets for Patricia's soul. She remembered everything.

Itaya was so anxious to find Mirza so he could continue his life with her, his sacred partner, his flame, as he so often told her.

***

At the Stasis Center, Mirza still hadn't woken up. It had already been a few days since they had all returned...

Itaya watched over her day and night. He consulted advisors with this kind of expertise, and they reassured him that this sometimes happened and that he shouldn't worry.

They had to treat her, and Itaya hoped with all her heart that she would regain consciousness. Then one day, stroking her forehead with his hand, Itaya sensed that Mirza had had a small start. Pleased, he prayed for her to open her eyes. A few minutes later, she did. Mirza wanted to sit down on her bunk. Itaya called her name. She looked at him with a big smile. He kissed her and asked her to go back to bed. He went to get one of the advisors to scan her. All was well. She could gradually resume her activities.

Both wonderfully happy, they couldn't help looking at each other and saying in chorus, as they did after every mission together:

"Special mission accomplished according to our divine plan."

Thank you to my readers for giving me your feedback and comments on my Amazon page. I read them all.

www.ingramcontent.com/pod-product-compliance
Lightning Source LLC
LaVergne TN
LVHW050314160826
845677LV00014B/3389

* 9 7 8 2 9 2 4 8 1 8 8 6 2 *